mcr

THE LITTLE WHITE HEN

The Little White Hen

First publication in
United States of America
Whittlesey House, a division
the McGraw-Hill Book Company, Inc., 1
Library of Cong
Catalog Card Number: 63-8
First published in Great Britain
The Bodley Head Ltd., 1
Text © Anita Hewett, 1
Illustrations © The Bodley Head Ltd., 1
Printed in Great Brit

Written by Anita Hewett

and drawn by William Stobbs

WHITTLESEY HOUSE McGraw-Hill Book Company, Inc.

NEW YORK TORONTO LONDON

4

Once upon a time a little white hen was scratching
in the farmyard, when she found a piece of paper,
covered all over with squiggly marks.

" Tuck-a-luck-luck," said the little white hen.
" It must be a letter. I wonder what it says."

The little white hen put on her spectacles.   But
she could not read the letter.

" I shall take it to the king. *He* knows everything."

5

Away she went through the woods towards the palace. In her little brown basket, tucked beneath her wing, was the letter.

After a time she met a fox.

"Good morning," said the fox. "I hope I see you well. And where are you going, on this fine, sunny morning?"

"I am taking a letter to the king, tuck-a-luck. Jump in my basket, and you can come, too. But your paws are rather muddy, so be careful, if you please."

The fox jumped into the little brown basket, and the little white hen went on her way.

After a time she came to a river.

" Good morning," said the river.
" I hope I see you well. And
where are you going, on this fine,
sunny morning ?"

" I am taking a letter to the king,
tuck-a-luck. Jump in my basket,
and you can come, too. But keep
yourself as dry as you can, if
you please."

The river ran into the little
brown basket, and the little white
hen went on her way.

After a time she came to a fire.

" Good morning," said the fire. " I hope
I see you well. And where are you going,
on this fine, sunny morning ?"

" I am taking a letter to the king,
tuck-a-luck. Jump in my basket, and you
can come, too. But cover yourself all over
with ashes, so that you do not burn me,
if you please."

The fire leapt into the little brown basket,
and the little white hen went on her way.

At last she came to the king's great palace. The soldier who was guarding the door looked down. He looked down, down, down at the little white hen, and he said in a loud voice: " Who are you ? And what have you brought in that little brown basket ?"

The little white hen was very frightened.

" Tuck-a-luck-a-letter. A letter for the king."

" Then come with me," the soldier said.

Tramp, tramp, tramp.   He marched through the palace.
The little white hen had to run, to keep up with him.

   She followed him on and on and on, and at last
they stood before the king.

   His voice seemed as loud as thunder as he said :
" What have you brought in that little
brown basket ?"

   " I have brought you a letter," said
the little white hen.   And she bowed
so low that she sat on the floor.

She took the letter out of the basket, and stretched on her toes to give it to the king. The fox had stood on it, and made muddy paw marks. The river had rested on it, and made damp patches. The fire had sat on it, and made little round holes with brown edges. There was hardly any writing to be seen.

" But this is just rubbish," shouted the king. " You are wasting my time with a dirty piece of paper. Soldier ! Take this hen away. Put her in the goose-run. I'll have her for my supper."

The little white hen picked up her basket, and the soldier picked up the little white hen. Tramp, tramp, tramp. He threw her in the goose-run.

The geese flew at the little white hen, and chased her.
The little white hen ran around and around.   She ran
so fast that she dropped the basket.

As the basket hit the ground the lid fell open, and out jumped the fox. He chased the geese everywhere — here, there, and everywhere. There was such a fuss and a flying of feathers that the soldier came in to see what had happened.

But he had left the gate of the goose-run open,
and the little white hen ran out of it quickly,
with the little brown basket tucked beneath
her wing.

" Catch her," called the soldier. " Catch
that hen."

Out of the palace ran the king, the queen, two
princesses, the cook and the kitchen maid, three little
page boys, and seven soldiers.   They all ran after the
little white hen.   Tuck-a-luck.

The little white hen was so dreadfully frightened that
she dropped her basket.   As it hit the ground the lid
fell open, and out ran the river.

The river spread deep and wide and shining,
and they all had to stop.

But the king sent the soldiers for boats, and the king, the queen, the two princesses, the cook and the kitchen maid, the three little page boys and the seven soldiers all rowed across the river.

The little white hen was far away in front, running through the woods that were near her home. But her poor little legs were tired, and the basket was heavy beneath her wing. Tuck-a-luck-luck. They were catching her up.

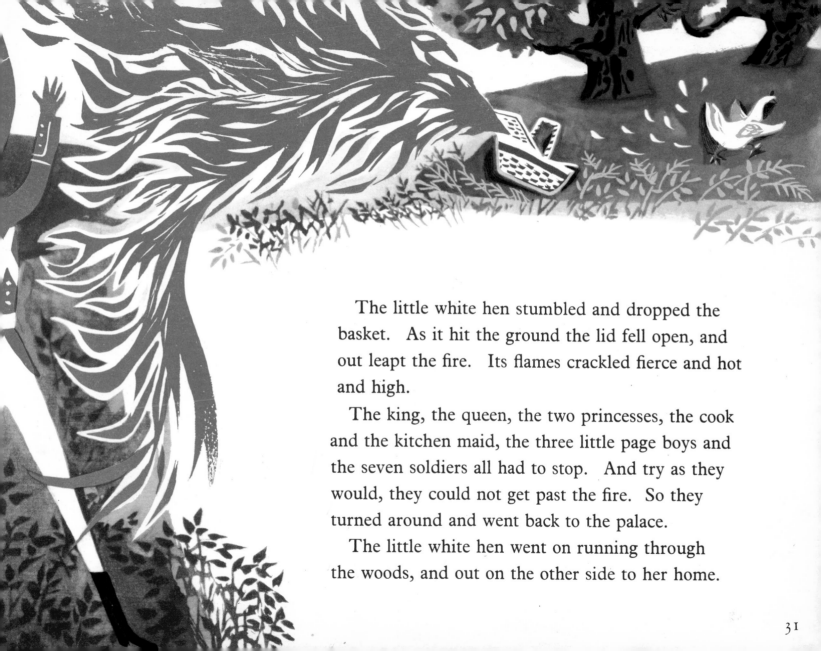

The little white hen stumbled and dropped the
basket. As it hit the ground the lid fell open, and
out leapt the fire. Its flames crackled fierce and hot
and high.

The king, the queen, the two princesses, the cook
and the kitchen maid, the three little page boys and
the seven soldiers all had to stop. And try as they
would, they could not get past the fire. So they
turned around and went back to the palace.

The little white hen went on running through
the woods, and out on the other side to her home.

But a strange and wonderful thing had happened.
The little white hen was white no longer. When the
fire had leapt out of the little brown basket, it had
scattered ashes, here, there, and everywhere.   Some of
them had fallen on the little white hen, and she was
a speckled hen, speckled from that day to this.

And her chickens were speckled, and her
chickens' chickens, too.